Cycle Star of Peeling Tower

CYCLE STAR
of
PEELING TOWER

Joan Eadington

Illustrated by Chris Ryley

AS TOLD IN JACKANORY BY
TINA HEATH

BRITISH BROADCASTING CORPORATION

By the same author:
The Adventures of Jonny Briggs
Jonny Briggs and the Great Razzle Dazzle
Jonny Briggs and the Giant Cave
Jonny Briggs and the Galloping Wedding
Jonny Briggs and the Jubilee Concert

Published by the
British Broadcasting Corporation
35 Marylebone High Street
London W1M 4AA

First published 1984
ISBN 0 563 20308 0
© Joan Eadington 1984

Phototypeset in 12/14 pt Linotron Baskerville
by Input Typesetting Ltd
and printed in England
by Hartnolls Ltd, Bodmin, Cornwall

Contents

1   The Find

"I've just found a bicycle at the back of Peeling Tower!" Kim was gasping with excitement. She looked at Andy in triumph. They spent quite a lot of time looking for treasure. Once they found an old bent metal jug full of cigarette cards in the long grass. And another time they found a cycle lamp that actually worked. Andy was glad about that. It was just what he wanted for his own bike.

"At first I thought it was a bit of scrap iron. Come and help me pull it up on to the path, Andy. Hurry . . . before mum gets back from work and wants to know what I'm doing." Kim's eyes sparkled at the thought of this marvellous mystery lying under the trees.

Peeling Tower where they both lived was a bit unusual. It wasn't a tower block. It was a small, very old tower – almost like a green lighthouse – with three floors and eight flats in it set in a small wood next to Barnfield housing estate and the shops.

But the all green paint was peeling off its golden sandstone. There were no fences round it – just long grass with a few coke tins and bits of broken milk bottle; and potato crisp packets were stuck in bushes alongside battered polythene trays from George's Take-Away.

If that sounds a bit gloomy, it wasn't, because on the other side of Peeling Tower was the countryside – with fields full of sheep and winding country lanes leading to the sea.

"How do you like living here?" said Andy as they picked their way along a bit of sandy, dried-up footpath surrounded by nettles and dock leaves.

"I like it a lot," said Kim, turning her face away because she suddenly felt a bit shy. "It's better than where me and mum was before. There was no one to play with, there. It's friendlier here."

Then, as she saw the bike again, she began to look anxious and almost sad. She was full of hope and fear all muddled up together. Hope – that the bike would be usable, and that somehow it could be hers for evermore. Yet fear – that it was indeed just a mangled bit of old scrap . . .

They pulled the bike to the path and Andy began to rub the mud off it. "It's almost like mine. It's a Rocket Racer! Mine cost pounds. Mum and dad had to pay for mine every week for two years."

They tried to wheel it. Its coppery-coloured frame gleamed in the sun. "The front wheel's buckled," said Andy, wiping a grimy hand across his dark hair. "It's been dumped."

But Kim never heard him . . . All she knew at this moment was that she, Kim Prestbury, had

found proper treasure at last. The sort of treasure she'd always wanted, always dreamed of . . . but had almost given up hope of ever getting.

For there was a reason she didn't think she'd ever get a bike, and the reason was sad: her father had been killed on a bike when she was a baby and her mother, Poppy, had a horror of them. Her mother would always say: "They're far too expensive", or, "There's nowhere to keep one," or, "It would scratch the door frames".

Suddenly Andy's cheerful voice broke into her thoughts. "Just think if we could mend it. We'd both have one then, and we could do all sorts. We could ride all the paths round Peeling Tower. We could go exploring to places where the buses don't go. We could go to places like River Island Castle where you have to be ferried across in the boat . . ."

Kim smiled back, slowly: "A bike of my own at last . . . Bike races, and trailing robbers . . . and balancing on one wheel. Maybe Mark Macdonald's dad would take us on some rides . . ."

"Maybe with him being a racing cyclist he'd even help us to mend it . . ." said Andy.

Because that was the first thing. Mending it was the first thing . . .

"There's another thing too," said Kim. "Where on earth could we keep it? My mum . . ." her voice faded sadly. At the moment she and her mum didn't seem to be getting on all that well because there'd been jam on one of the door handles and a mysterious patch of grease on the wallpaper – just at a time when her mum was trying to get the flat looking good.

So every day when Kim's mum rushed out to work she'd say: "Don't touch anything whilst I'm out. Don't be late for school. Don't get butter on the wallpaper again, and don't eat all the jam." And if Kim or Andy ever said it was a nice sunny day she would say something like: "Rain is on the cards – with *giant* hailstones."

"Perhaps Mr Proud would look after it for us," said Andy. (Mr Proud lived in a flat near Andy. He was a retired ship's engineer and lived alone with a brown and orange cat called Bubbles.)

"Let's try Mark's flat, first," said Kim.

But when they got to Mark's – their luck was out. No sign of Mark, his baby sister – or anyone . . . Mark was six. His sister Jan was two.

"There's no sign of the van outside either," said Andy. "They'll have gone to the Saturday cycle track event at the Sports Stadium."

Mark Macdonald lived on the ground floor. There were no lifts in Peeling Tower, so by the time Kim and Andy hauled the bike up the stone steps to Mr Proud's they were quite breathless.

There was a brass door-knocker on his front door. It was shaped like a leaping fish. Kim lifted it nervously. What would he say? "Please let him take it to look after," she prayed. "Please let me be able to have a bike of my own – even if it has

to stay in someone else's home and be kept a secret."

The door opened. Mr Proud was standing there in a thick blue chunky-knit cardigan. He stared first at them and then at the bike leaning against the wall.

"Please could you mind this bike for us, Mr Proud?" said Kim, feeling all quavery. Her voice began to go faint.

Mr Proud scratched his bald head slowly: "It's a bit of a wreck isn't it? All top show and tin if you ask me . . ."

"It never is!" said Kim. "It's a *bicycle*. It only needs the wheel straightening and the chain . . ." The words began to choke up. How could they possibly get it working without some help and somewhere to keep it?

"A bicycle?" scoffed Mr Proud. "And you want *me* to keep this fantastic bit of bent scrap iron in my neat little hallway blocking everything up and trapping people's shins and bruising their poor ankles? So what's wrong with your own establishments?"

"I've already got a bike – " said Andy.

"True . . . True . . ." said Mr Proud. "How did you get on in that there Cycling Proficiency Test?"

"I passed it!"

"Good. Good." He turned to Kim: "And what about you?"

"I haven't got a bike yet. That's why . . . This is for – "

"It's for her, Mr Proud – but her mum won't – "

"Won't what?" said Mr Proud bluntly.

"She's not very keen on me having one," said Kim miserably as she put her hand lovingly on the handlebars.

"Then you can't have one can you?" said Mr Proud unfeelingly. "If mum says 'no' – then it's no. And where did you get it anyway?"

Kim's eyes were stinging with disappointment. She couldn't even answer in case she sounded as if she was crying. She began to lift the bike away from the wall.

"Come on then," said Andy, "we'll put it back where we found it dumped; in the long grass behind the tower . . ."

"Wait." Mr Proud was looking at them like someone with a secret plan tucked away in his mind: "How about *giving* me that bike for a birthday present? It's my birthday tomorrow and I'm sixty-eight . . ."

Their mouths fell open in startled surprise! "It wouldn't do for you, Mr Proud. It's much too small – and it's broken. It just wouldn't do as a *birthday present* . . ." Kim and Andy gave each other a quick puzzled look.

"No need to look so amazed. Perhaps your poor old junk heap's looking for a nice peaceful home to recover in. And perhaps – when my birthday's over I'll pass it back to *you* as a present – when you've got things sorted out a bit . . ."

"You mean you'll look after it for us, and pretend it's a present?"

Mr Proud gave a long plain look across the tops of their heads – just as if he were looking far out to sea: "Thank you for your present," he said solemnly. "Put it in the hall and mind you don't tread on the cat."

Kim's face shone with happiness: "Many happy returns of tomorrow, Mr Proud. Will you be getting any more presents?"

"Bubbles might buy me a bit of fish for her tea," he smiled. Then he said: "You can both come to my party if you want. Four o'clock start. Plenty of food. Tell everyone."

"I wonder who did dump the bike?" said Andy, after they'd thanked Mr Proud for his invitation and gone downstairs again.

"What does it matter?" said Kim excitedly. "All I want now is for mum to let me take it home." Her face was flushed with happiness. "If mum lets me keep it – I'll become a Superstar. I'll go racing round the WORLD. I'll wear a leather crash helmet and shoes with metal pedal grips and pants with a fleecy padded bit to stop my bottom getting saddle sore – like proper cyclists wear. We could have a club and race round Peeling Tower."

Andy nodded and jumped in the air waving his

fist. "I'd win! But I'll help you to practise. It'd
be great. That is . . . if your mum – " he hesitated.

Kim's face clouded over again: "If, if, if . . ."
she said dolefully.

"Certainly not!" said Kim's mum, Poppy, after
tea. "My cream carpet just won't stand it. No,
no, a thousand times *no*! Why must you go on
about it?" Her eyebrows looked like two black furry
caterpillars about to have a fight and her short
hair looked extra spiky. Then she said, "And
anyway, you haven't even got a bike so why all
this fuss?"

"It was just supposing I had . . ." said Kim.
"Just supposing I *found one* or anything . . ."

"Found one?" Poppy looked suspicious. "How
could you find one? Bicycles usually belong to
someone."

"If it was just a scrappy one that could be
mended?" Her mother ignored her. It was
hopeless . . . "It's Mr Proud's birthday
tomorrow," Kim went on. "He's having a party.
We can all go."

"Who said?"

"He did. He told me and Andy." Then she said
very quickly, almost in one breath: "If Kerrie
Thomas lived in this top flat she'd have a long
rope made of sheets and she'd haul her bike up
and down the outside of Peeling Tower like a real
adventure. She said if *I* had a bike she'd help me

to do it any time – just in case the steps were blocked or anything."

"Kerrie Thomas gets too much of her own way," shouted her mum as Kim ran from the room. "Come back and wipe this door handle! Mr Pickling's coming round later on and there's nothing worse than sticky door handles . . ."

The next day when Kim met Andy to go to the party, she said: "Mum just doesn't want me to *ever* have any fun or adventures. All she thinks about is her cream carpet and that new friend of hers, Mr Pickling."

"Cheer up," said Andy as they hurried to Mr Proud's front door.

The small flat was packed with people. There were birthday cards everywhere, and balloons and huge vases of flowers. Everyone was talking and laughing. Mrs Pink, the retired school nurse, was giving out sausage rolls and cups of tea. Miss Grigg's purple beads had snapped and she was crawling about looking for them and her friend Mrs Lord was undoing her belt to eat another iced bun. Little Granny Thomas was there, too. She was known as ' "A Living Miracle" '. She was Kerrie Thomas's Great Grandma, and she was talking to Mr and Mrs Bosky. Mr Bosky was an insurance agent. He had a computer chess set. He and Mrs Bosky had six grown-up children who lived all over the world in places like Australia and Hong Kong.

When everyone had sung *Happy Birthday*, and Mr Proud had blown out sixty-eight pink and blue candles, he came over to Kim. "I've had to move the bike for a bit," he whispered. "Mr and Mrs Bosky are looking after it. It's on Mr Bosky's allotment in his hut."

"What was he whispering to you about?" asked Kerrie, trying to lick ice-cream off the tip of her nose.

"He was telling us where he's keeping the present we bought him . . ."

"You mean that old wreck of a bike your mum won't let – "

"Sh . . ." Kim glared. Trust Kerrie to broadcast it! She had red hair and was always giving away people's deepest secrets in a loud voice, accidentally on purpose.

"Why don't you get that old Tin Lizzie up to your flat whilst your mum's at work; you could stick it under your bed. Then you could mend it when she wasn't there."

"Take no notice of her, Kim," said Andy. "It would never fit under your bed. And how could you mend it in a place full of white carpets?" Andy glared at Kerrie: "You wouldn't dare if it was your flat. You're always telling people to do things you wouldn't dare to do yourself . . ."

"I never am!"

"Oh yes you are . . ."

"Watch out Andy Crabshaw – unless you want

this salmon sandwich down your neck . . ."

"What on earth are you three plotting?" said Mr Proud looking hard at the salmon sandwich which had flown out of Kerrie's hand. But he didn't really expect an answer, because he was thinking of the special plan he'd just worked out. "I've been talking to the others and we've all decided to have an outing," he said. "We're going to hire a minibus. Any ideas on a good place to go?"

There was an amazed silence. Peeling Tower had never had an outing before.

"One thing that struck me as a good start was if we went to give Mark's dad a bit of support at the Lake Cycle Race next month. There's lots going on up there. Cafés, sailing boats, tree swings, nature trails, gift shops, pubs . . . fresh air . . . good scenery. What more could we want? He says he'll help you to put that bike right, Kim. You're in luck."

A day out to a real cycle race! Kim was over the moon with delight. And as they left the party she said to Andy: "Mark's dad might win! He once had his picture in 'Cycling' magazine . . . I wish *I* could be a star rider like that." Then her face clouded and she said: "Suppose mum won't let me go . . .?"

"I hope she does," said Andy, "because if your mum lets you – my mum'll let me . . ."

"I'll be going," shouted Kerrie Thomas. "And

my granny'll definitely go. She'll go anywhere and do *anything*. She's a living miracle . . ."

"I wish my mum was a living miracle, too," thought Kim as she climbed up all the steps to her own home in the top flat. "I wish she would go anywhere and do anything . . . Please change her to a living miracle – just for a short while . . . just for this one outing." Then she stopped thinking about living miracles and started climbing the stairs two at a time dreaming of all the good things to come when she finally made it . . . when she became the Cycle Star of Peeling Tower.

2   Strange Surprise

The Macdonalds had a bit more space on the bottom floor of Peeling Tower. They had a little square room with lots of windows where Mark's dad – Wally – looked after his bikes.

Wally had three bikes: one old one he had done up from a frame he found lying on a rubbish tip. He added new bits to it (or rather – second-hand bits), and painted it all dark blue. He went to work on this one. Then he had a silvery-coloured sports bike for practising, and also for doing long training runs. And finally, he had his very best bike. The one he used for racing. It had been built for him by his friend Jack who owned a cycle shop, and it was painted bright blue and yellow.

Kim and Andy could hardly get in the room when they took the Rocket Racer to be mended. The place was full of bike wheels and chains and bike spokes, and long, lank-looking, loopy tubular bicycle tyres – all skinny looking – known as "tubs".

"Give it here then – and let's have a gander,"

said Wally as he lifted Rocket Racer on to his bench. "Yes, it needs a good straightening out – and a new front wheel – no doubt about that. I'll see if Jack's got a small spare wheel tucked away in his shop. How does that suit?"

They were so pleased they were dumbstruck. They smiled back happily. "Soon we'll be able to go on loads and loads of adventures . . . Both of us . . . on our *own* bikes," breathed Kim.

And it almost seemed that everything was right at last, for Wally had it mended in next to no time, and in next to no time Kim and Andy were skimming round Peeling Tower like a pair of swallows on wheels . . . but only . . . only when Kim's mum was at work.

"I'll tell you what we could do today," said Kim a couple of days after Wally had mended the bicycle, "we could ride along the sea road to that shop that sells everything, and see if we could get a present for Wally, for mending the bike. But first I'll have to get the money out of my piggy-bank. There isn't much – but it's better than nothing . . ."

Kim's piggy bank was a large pot pig with blue flowers on it. It stood on the living-room mantelpiece where everyone could see it. Often you had to get a blunt knife to help the money out as there was no other opening, but today, because there wasn't much in it, the money toppled out easily on to the table; mostly twopenny

pieces, but here and there a twenty pence . . .

"We'll make him a 'Thank You' card as well,"
said Kim.

They found a piece of white card from a box
and cut out a rectangle. Then they folded it like
a greetings card and wrote THANK YOU
WALLY on it in felt-tipped pen, and Andy drew
a man in a track suit – because he liked drawing.

"We can put it in the bag with the present,"
said Kim.

The sea road was very quiet on Saturday
mornings out of holiday time. There were no
turnings off it, and no houses leading on to it. It
was ideal for racing. The two of them raced like
the wind. Kim felt the salt spray from the sea

against her cheeks. Her eyes were screwed into
narrow slits against the sharp sea breeze. Andy
was well ahead. Andy was always ahead . . . She
pedalled quicker and harder and gradually, very
gradually, she began to catch up, until by the
time they got near The Everything Shop they were
equal.

"It's only because I slowed down a bit to let
you catch up," gasped Andy as they flopped off
their bikes. Kim smiled. She didn't say anything,
but she knew . . . she *knew* she was getting better
and better.

"Something for a racing cyclist?" Mrs Bland
who owned The Everything Shop looked
flummoxed. "It's a new one on me . . . Would

cycle batteries be any good? But there again I don't suppose they race much in the dark do they? How about a sponge to wipe the sweat off his face then . . . or a bottle of linament to rub on his legs? I've a feeling they swamp themselves with things like camphorated oil."

Then Andy had an idea: "Mint cake," he said. "One of those bars of mint cake. It's very sweet and it gives you lots of energy."

Kim put out her money. She had just enough for a large block of mint cake. It was a bit like white chocolate only it was more sugary looking and it had a blue picture on its white wrapper.

"Can you put it in a big paper bag please Mrs Bland, so that we can put a card in with it?"

She found them a bag with leaves and flowers printed all over it. The mint cake looked just like a real present.

"For *me*?" said Wally in amazement when they got back and gave it to him. "How did you find out I liked mint cake? Thanks a lot."

"Isn't it great that everything's turning out right?" said Kim. And when her mum came back from work that evening even she noticed a change . . .

"What have you been doing today, then?" she asked.

"Just playing . . . playing with Andy. But we had a great time. We raced each other . . ."

Her mother looked thoughtful: "I'm sorry I'm

not always here on Saturdays. I wish I didn't have to work such awkward hours . . ." Then she looked at the piggy-bank on the mantelpiece and said: "See if you can find me a ten-pence piece – I'm just going to give Mr Pickling a ring, at the box. I wish we were on the phone . . ."

Kim's heart stood still. The piggy-bank. How could she get ten pence from it when it was empty? "There aren't any in it, mum."

"Aren't any in it? Are you *sure*? I saw you put one in last week out of your pocket money. Bring it here and tip it out on to the table."

With sinking hopes . . . Kim slowly took the piggy-bank . . . What would she say when her mum realised it was empty? It would mean that the bike would be a secret no longer . . . because her mother was the world's best at finally rooting out the truth.

But Kim didn't want it to be like that – she wanted the truth to come out in a better, more gradual, way – so that her mum would be kind and sympathetic.

"Hurry up then," said her mum impatiently. Then – glory of glories – her mum grabbed her own handbag. "Waiting for you to tip that thing out's like waiting for the man in the moon," she said. "There's one here . . ." And she hurried away to the phone box.

Kim felt weak at the knees. When would this awful secret about the bike be out in the open so that she didn't have to worry any more?

"You're always wanting to go *somewhere*," said her mother a couple of days later. "I think Mr Proud's got a cheek – getting you and Andy to put those notices through everyone's door, about this outing."

"But it's for *all* of us . . ." said Kim pleadingly. "We can go, too. You could bring Mr Pickling."

"Ronald isn't the least interested in Mark Macdonald's father *or* cycle races. If Ronald and I want to go on an outing we'll go in Ronald's own car – not a rickety old mini-bus."

"It's not rickety! It's new! Even Granny Thomas is going. She said if she was sixty years younger she'd be in the cycle race with Wally herself."

"She's just being silly," said Kim's mum as she hastily shook a rug out of the window. "Girls don't go in cycle races. They're not strong enough."

"They do just! What about Beryl Burton and Mandy Jones?" Kim could see her mum didn't even *want* to know. "Beryl Burton's been a champion tons of times, Wally said."

"Wally . . .? And who's Wally?"

"Mr Macdonald."

"Then in future please call him Mr Macdonald."

"But they call him Wally in the cycle races. And you call Mark's mum Sylvia . . ."

"Stop being *cheeky*. You're far too big for your boots my child . . ."

Kim relapsed into mournful silence. She hadn't even got a proper answer about going on the outing.

"What did she say?" said Andy eagerly when they met again. "Is she going to let you go on it? I can – if you can . . ."

Kim brushed her hand quickly across her eyes. "She's just not interested. She didn't even know who Beryl Burton was. I expect if Mr Pickling told her something she'd soon remember it . . ." She pulled a crumpled pink tissue from her sleeve and blew her nose very loud. "She *loves* Mr Pickling. Loves him more than anyone . . ."

"It's better than not loving anyone at all," said Andy, trying to be helpful.

"But if only she'd let me do exciting things like cycling and parachuting and – "

"Not all at once . . ." said Andy slowly. "No one can do everything at once. Just imagine if you were like me with a baby brother and sister pulling you to bits all the time. James chewed my real footballer's autograph yesterday, then spat it out all over the floor. And this morning Debby dribbled over my best picture of a cricket bat and it went all smudgy."

Then he said: "Let's ask Mr Proud if he can persuade your mum and Mr Pickling to come on the trip."

Later that night as Kim lay in bed, she kept hoping that Mr Proud would come to her rescue. She even tried to keep awake in the hope of him coming round to the flat. But soon it was morning – and there was her mum – tugging at her and telling her to get up.

"I've got a nice surprise for you dear . . . so hurry up."

A nice surprise? Kim blinked and yawned. She stared at her mother's beaming face. It must be something good to make her look like that.

Quickly she got ready and went in the kitchen for her breakfast.

"And now for my news . . ." said her mum, splashing the milk in a carefree manner over a couple of Weetabix.

Kim hardly dared to breathe. What a wonderful treat if Mr Proud had called last night and persuaded her mother to go on the trip. Mr Pickling, her mum, and most of all – herself . . . And lots and lots of cycle racing, nature trails, cups of tea, orange squash, ice-cream, chocolate cake! Surely her mother would like all that?

Then – if everyone was still in a good mood she'd be able to mention Rocket Racer at last – and about it being in the hut on Mr Bosky's allotment – and about how she – Kim Prestbury – intended to grow up and be a star cycling champion.

"Someone came to see me last night when you

were asleep, dear . . . Someone you know quite well. But this time it was rather special . . ."

Kim waited while her mum took a small bit of toast. She heard every crackle and crunch. It seemed to be hours – but she didn't mind. She felt happy at last. Good old Mr Proud . . .

A crumb of toast caught in Poppy's throat and she gave a slight cough. Then she smiled at her daughter: "It was Mr Pickling who popped in. He brought us the best surprise of our lives . . ."

Kim was startled. Mr Pickling? The best surprise of their lives? How could *he* do that? She suddenly went a bit cold . . . What was it? Whatever could it be? The trouble was that most times the things her *mum* thought were great weren't the things *she* thought were great. Sometimes they were the exact opposite. Supposing then, that this was something terrible instead of something terrific?

"The fact is, Kim, your Uncle Ronald has asked me to marry him."

"My Uncle Ronald?" stammered Kim in a shocked daze. "B-but he's not my uncle. You always told me to call him Mr – "

"It's all different now," said her mum hastily. "You'll be able to call him Uncle – just like Andy's Uncle Fred."

"If it's all different – does it mean you and Mr – I mean Uncle Ronald – will be able to come on the trip?"

"We might . . . It all depends on Ronald. We shall be getting married in June and you can be my bridesmaid . . ."

A bridesmaid . . . Surely her mother knew she wasn't interested in *those*. "Will he be coming to live here?"

"We aren't quite sure yet. I must get to work now. Don't be late for school, my angel," her mother gave her a happy kiss, "and don't get butter on the wallpaper again. Goodbye dear. Be a good girl."

That day when Kim and Andy were coming home from school, Kim said: "So they *might* come on the trip after all . . ."

"They might? Yipppeeeeee!" yelled Andy. "You might be quite lucky after all." They stared at each other and their eyes glowed with happiness.

When Kim got in she was surprised to find her mother and Uncle Ronald already there. The tea was almost ready – and there were ham sandwiches with all the crusts cut off and bits of parsley on top. A special tea . . .

Uncle Ronald smiled at her: "You know the good news then?"

Kim nodded: "Yes. Mum says you might both be able to come on the outing to the cycle race after all."

"Not *that* news . . ." her mother sighed. "He means about us getting – "

"What's the other news then?" asked Uncle

Ronald, eating ten small sandwiches in ten gollops and having two lots of strawberry jelly and cream.

"We're all going on an outing from Peeling Tower to watch Mark Macdonald's dad in a cycle race and there'll be lots of other things to do as well . . . adventurous things . . ."

"She keeps going on and on about it, Ronald," said Poppy giving him a long look as she handed him about a quarter of chocolate swiss roll all in one go. "Travelling in an awful old mini-bus, they are. Not my cup of tea. Give me some good shops any day . . ."

Kim's eyes began to smart – then to her surprise she heard Uncle Ronald say in a gentle joking tone: "We've a lifetime to look at shops. Let's go on this trip with Kim. I'm sick of always driving the car. We can take cushions if the mini-bus is a bit hard."

Her mother looked stunned. "Are you quite *sure*, Ronald? Will you *like* cycle racing and nature trails?" her voice weakened.

"Like them? 'Course I shall. A nice change. Something fresh." He smiled at Kim and she smiled back. She stared at him hard after that – when he wasn't looking. He was very big with brown bushy hair and a bright green pullover. Sandwiches with the crusts cut off were far too small for him. And he even needed three mugs of tea instead of one. But suddenly she was glad he

was coming to live with them . . .

"Did you ever climb trees or anything when you were little, Uncle Ronald?"

"Climb trees?" A huge smile spread across his face. "There was this huge tree in our park with branches almost down to the ground and you could climb it like a ladder to the top of the sky . . ."

Kim sighed with happy relief. She began to explain about the trip and how Mr Proud had organised it. She explained it all. All except one thing . . . the rocket racer – back once again in Mr Proud's hall waiting for the moment of truth; waiting for its real owner to come forward and claim it: – the cycle star of Peeling Tower . . . But when . . .? When on earth would it be?

3   The Give-away

"It seems strange to think that mum doesn't even know I can ride a bike . . ." thought Kim as she rode back home with Andy and Wally.

Wally had taken them for a training run to River Island Castle. They had to leave their bikes at a farm. Then they had to go along a narrow path with wooden fences along the sides of fields, and the path had twelve small gates like wooden turnstiles.

"It's a bit of an obstacle race isn't it?" Wally had said. "A good job we didn't bring our bikes and have to lift them over every one all the way to the castle!"

To get across to the castle they had to ring a bell. Wally pulled this rope and a brass bell above it began to clang. Then a man rowed across from the castle to the wooden jetty where they were waiting and rowed them across.

The castle was very old and grim and dark-looking, with a high square tower and huge

dungeons where they used to keep prisoners.

As they pedalled back home again, Kim thought of all the good times she'd had since the bike arrived in her life. What a thrill it was when she first learned to keep her balance without falling off – or having to put her feet on the ground, that moment when she found she could go on and on without overbalancing. What delight! What freedom!

But still there was a nagging sadness about her mother not knowing.

Even Wally didn't know that her mother didn't know – or he would never have taken them out.

"I hope it's a good day tomorrow too, for our outing," she said to Andy.

And it was! Mr Proud's day was perfect.

The windows of the green and white mini-bus sparkled as mums, dads, uncles, aunts, neighbours and children clambered inside for the Lake Cycle Race.

"This straw hat of mine is fifty years old," said Granny Thomas. "It's as good as when I first bought it."

"Because there's never enough sun in this country for it to get worn out," remarked Mr Bosky cheerfully. "I've had these sun-glasses for twenty years."

Mark Macdonald and his mother and baby sister had gone in their own car with Wally because Wally had to be there extra early.

"He has to have his bike checked over," said Kim to Kerrie Thomas. "You aren't allowed to enter any races unless you've got your crash hat and licence." She began to count all the riders' names on the programme of events. "There are thirty-three people in it. I hope Wally wins! He's number sixteen."

Kerrie smiled, and for once was silenced by such an amount of information, while Andy nodded happily and rubbed his hand gently across his camera. He was lucky to be taking it. His mother was always frightened he would lose it. She had been to see Kim's mum to make sure everything would be all right.

"Are you actually *going* then?" she said to Poppy in astonishment. "I can't possibly come. I'm always in such a rush. I *must* dash round to mother's for a knitting pattern for quick-knit wool. And I've *got* to fly to my sister's at the same time. I shall have to whisk James and Debbie into the push chair and just *gallop* . . . Life seems to rush by . . ."

Soon the bus was speeding along roads and motorways towards the lake. Then it stopped at some toilets in a wooded lay-by.

"There's a scent of bracken and pine needles," said Andy picking up a pine cone and sniffing it: "What did your mum bring for eats?"

"Stacks and stacks. It's much better having Uncle Ronald with us. Because he eats so much, we all get more. We've even got bananas and chocolate biscuits and strawberry yoghurts. There's plenty for you, too."

"I've got cream crackers and cheese and an apple and a packet of crisps – and money for a fruit drink," said Andy.

When they were all back in the bus again, Noel the driver counted them. "There's nothing worse than leaving some poor soul trapped in the toilets," he said.

And soon the whole bus began to sing "Oh dear what can the matter be – three old ladies were locked in the lavatree . . ." until a rival group of more respectable people like Poppy and Mrs Bosky started up with "One man and his dog – went to mow a meadow . . ." which lasted for ever. And by then they'd reached the start of the cycle race and the Log Cabin Café.

There was a changing room for the cyclists at the back of the café. It was bright and busy with gleaming sports bikes and riders in their club colours. Kim saw Wally ride to the starting line of the race in a red, white and yellow jersey with green sleeves and the words SILVER SANDS CC written on it.

There were people in the race from all over the country.

Everyone waited excitedly while a man in a brown jacket and blue tracksuit trousers gave all the racers a warning talk about taking care and keeping to the correct side of the road. And obeying road safety rules at all times.

"They're away!" yelled Kim. The air was filled with cheers and shouts. A smell of wintergreen which the cyclists had rubbed on their legs to keep their muscles trim, wafted everywhere.

"Thank God they've gone . . ." said Poppy to
Uncle Ronald. She was shivering slightly. Poppy
had needed courage to force herself to come and
watch men on racing bikes – after what had
happened to her own husband, all those years ago.

Uncle Ronald squeezed her hand comfortingly
as the great, whirring, pedalling mass of brightly-
coloured bodies zoomed far into the distance along

the flat, sparkling granite road. Then Kim's mum and Uncle Ronald disappeared into the nearest gift shop.

But for Kim and Andy it was different. They went along the road and found a really good look-out point where they could see the course winding round up and over the hills for miles. And Mr Proud lent them his binoculars.

Then Mr Proud helped Andy to get his camera ready to take a photo of the race when it came round again on the next lap.

"Six times round . . ." shouted Kim. "I wish I was in it! I wish we could have a race round Peeling Tower . . ."

"They're here *again*," called Andy. "I can see the lead car with its lights on!"

And soon Kim saw it too. It was white, and had a large board on top saying CYCLE RACE IN PROGRESS. A huge bunch of racing cyclists streamed along behind it.

But where was Wally?

It had all been so quick that they hadn't seen a sign of him!

"Nineteen minutes to do seven miles," said Mr Proud. "Seven miles of steep hills and long winding roads."

And soon they were all round again – but this time it was different. There was a break in the group. There were three people well in front and one was number sixteen . . .

"WALLY . . . Come on Wally . . . keep going . . ."

The third time round Wally was still in the first three . . . but this time the rest of the bunch were catching up and narrowing the gap.

Could Wally really stay at the front for the whole of the race? Supposing he had a burst tyre . . . or his spokes broke . . . or . . . Everyone was going mad with excitement.

As the race came round for the fourth time their spirits sank a bit. Wally was no longer in the front three. He was back in the bunch. And there was a big gap between the bunch and the four front racers who were speeding along in single file.

"He'll *never* catch up again, now," said Kim.

"Only two more laps to go," shouted Andy. "And only three pictures left on my film. Come on Silver Sands . . ."

Eagerly they watched the lead car arriving again, and *this* time Wally was in a group of seven riders at the very front and they were one minute ahead of the rest of the bunch!

"Someone from that bunch of seven will be the winner," said Mr Proud. "Come on. Let's get back to the finishing line to cheer them. You've got to be tough to be a racing cyclist!"

Even Kim's mum and Uncle Ronald were there to see the final sprint . . . although Poppy did sometimes look away a bit as if she didn't really like to watch . . .

Everyone else craned their necks and stared hard along the road to see who would be the first cyclist to appear after the lead car. Soon a small speeding figure on a slim silvery machine grew

larger and larger. He shot at terrific speed in a furious wobbling movement towards the finishing line. And two more followed him – racing each other in a mad fight for second place, across the finishing mark on the road.

But not one of the three was Wally . . .

Ah well . . .

"He's here! He's here!" cried Andy. "He's racing all the others!" Along came Wally – going like the clappers for fourth place with only a few seconds gap.

"Good old Wally," shouted everyone as he took his hands from the handlebars and gave a victory wave of his arms.

"Didn't he do well?" said Granny Thomas. "He makes me proud to be living in Peeling Tower." Then she said to Mr Bosky: "Don't they have any bicycle bells?"

"It was terrific," said Mr Proud when they were all back in the bus again. Everyone agreed with him, even Kim's mum.

All the way back home Kim wondered whether to just say something about bicycles for schoolgirls . . . to get her mum warmed up to the idea . . . but she just didn't dare.

And then the ice broke. It was quite by accident.

In a loud voice, above the hum of the mini-bus, Andy said: "I wonder if your Rocket Racer would ever go at that speed, Kim . . ."

"Kim's Rocket Racer? Whatever's that when it's

at home . . .?" demanded Poppy, sharply.

There was a sudden silence from the back row of the bus as Andy realised what he'd said. The silence made Kim's mum even more suspicious and she turned to Ronald and said: "Do *you* know what it is, Ronald?"

Uncle Ronald was just dozing off. He blinked hurriedly. "Rocket Racer . . . no idea, love. Speed boat? Racing car perhaps?"

"*I* know what it is . . ." shouted Kerrie Thomas, who thought it was a quiz game. "It's Kim's bike she found on the tip! The one Wally mended for her. The one Mr Proud's keeping till she can take it home!"

Kim went all weak and pale. The dreaded secret was out at last . . . not all smoothly and gently but in one big awful shock! What would her mum say? The fat was on the fire . . . her mother would never forgive her for deceiving her. And she would hate Mr Proud too for being mixed up in it all . . . She clutched the side of the bus seat fearfully.

Then – to her utter amazement, she heard Uncle Ronald say: "I didn't know Kim was lucky enough to have a sports bike, Poppy. It must have been quite a triumph – reclaiming it from a rubbish tip."

"It must indeed," said her mum grimly. "And if I know anything about it – it'll go back there! I shan't say anything to Mr Proud about it *today*, as I don't want to spoil this outing. But believe me,

I shall have *more* than a word with him when I get back from work tomorrow." Her face was an angry pink.

"What a perfect day out! Thank you very much for organising it all, Mr Proud," said everyone as they stepped out into the warm summery air outside Peeling Tower a bit later.

"It was a pleasure. I like being kept busy. Nice to see how the other half lives from time to time . . . I think I'll try racing round the tower myself – on my birthday present!" He smiled at Kim and gave her a wink.

But her mum wasn't smiling or winking. She said "Can I call in and see you about something, tomorrow evening, Mr Proud?" Her voice was cold and stabbing as an icicle.

"Sure you can Poppy. Any time." His sounded warm and friendly.

Then Poppy turned to Kim: "And I'll see *you*, young lady – when we're alone. There seems to be a lot to talk about."

Kim's spirits sank to their lowest ebb. She could already see the scene; could hear her mother's voice full of accusation, rising higher and higher as she found out about all the deceit; could see herself standing there pleading for forgiveness with tears running down her cheeks. That was the way it always was when there was a scene with her mother.

As Kim and Poppy and Uncle Ronald climbed the steps leading to the top flat Kim made a secret wish on every step. And they were all about happy endings for Rocket Racer. Happy endings and new beginnings in a proper home. A home fit for her own bicycle to live in. And a hope that her mother would understand and listen when she tried to explain.

On the way to school the next day, she said to Andy: "Mum and I had a heck of a row last night over the bike. I wish her visit to Mr Proud was all over and done with . . ." She looked sadly at the row of lock-up concrete garages they were passing, next to Peeling Tower. There were six of them. Two of them always seemed empty. The doors were scratched and rusty and uncared for.

"If I could keep it in one of those . . ." breathed Kim. "If only we could find out who owns them and if there's space inside."

Andy nodded. Then they stopped wishing and began to run to the main road to join all their friends tracking their way towards the green playing fields and pale blue railings of the Queen Elizabeth Primary school.

The minute she returned from work, Poppy was round to Mr Proud's flat – with the words Rocket Racer trembling on her lips and Kim dragging behind her. Mr Proud's brass door knocker got a real pounding.

"Hold on!" he gasped as he came hurrying down from the second floor, because he wasn't in his flat at all. "Whatever's happened? The noise sounds bad. Don't give me any really sad news or it'll disturb the coffee and cream éclairs I've been enjoying with Miss Grigg and Mrs Lord."

Then he opened his front door and stopped joking: "Come in, come in," he said gently. "Don't just *stand* there. What can I do for you? You both look very solemn." He gave Poppy a shrewd look. He didn't often see her on a working weekday.

Her mum saw the bike immediately as it lay in proud copper glory against the primrose-coloured wallpaper in Mr Proud's hall.

The words Rocket Racer in red and gold seemed to sing . . .

"We meet at last." said Poppy with an angry smile. "*This* . . . is *it* . . . I take it?" She stared at the bike.

There was silence.

"Kim has been very deceitful to keep it all a secret. And, quite frankly, Mr Proud – I don't think *you* are much better for helping her. I should have been the first person to know about it. But instead, I'm the last!"

Kim hung her head in shame. It was a funny sort of shame really. She didn't feel sorry or remorseful for herself. She felt sorry and ashamed that her mother had trounced poor Mr Proud when all along he'd been so kind and helpful about the bike. But to her amazement he didn't seem in the least upset. All he said was: "Relax, Poppy – and I'll put the kettle on."

"Don't 'Poppy' me . . ." exclaimed Kim's mum angrily. "It's no use trying to butter *my* paws . . ." Then she cooled down a bit and said: "All right then Percy, I will have a cup. But no sugar and very weak."

Mr Proud poured her out a cup of weak tea. The cup had a curly gold edge. He gave Kim some orange squash with ice cubes in it, and a biscuit. "About this bike, then . . ." he said.

"About this bike. Yes!" said Poppy, setting her lips in a firm line.

"It's mine at present . . ." Mr Proud looked at her calmly. "I'm its owner. Some very kind children gave it to me for a birthday present. Mind you – I did rather push them into it . . ." He spread his hands towards the bike: "But as you can guess – it's a bit small. Ideally, more the size for someone like . . . er . . . Kim, for instance?" He sighed sadly: "But I believe her mother isn't keen on the idea?"

"Not in the least keen," said Poppy firmly. "Bicycles have never done me a scrap of good. I never had one as a child. And I don't intend to clutter up the flat with one at this time in life." She drew her breath painfully: "And I expect you know about . . . about . . ." the words seemed to dry up . . . "Kim's father?"

Mr Proud nodded: "I know . . . I know it's very hard for you. It was a terrible loss. But you can't let it spoil Kim's life." He handed her the plate of biscuits.

Kim's mother took a chocolate one and began to nibble it slowly, because she was thinking about what Mr Proud had said.

"Whilst I was upstairs just now, talking to Miss Grigg and Mrs Lord," said Mr Proud, "I asked them about those two empty garages . . ."

"Those garages?" Kim's mum gulped her tea. Her grey eyes looked grey and sparky – like crackling fireworks.

"Who is it owns those two at the end of the row, Poppy? Do you – or I, does anyone else know? They've been like that for ten years – ever since I came to live here. It seems a damned shame to me. What a waste . . . All empty-looking, and boarded up . . ."

At last Kim's mother began to melt. "Funnily enough Ronald was asking about them the other day. I expect you know we're getting married in June? Well, of course – if *he* comes to live here – he's going to need a place for his car and we were wondering about those garages . . ."

"Me too," said Mr Proud smiling. "I wouldn't mind sharing some space in one. I could do with proper space for a work-bench. A garage like one of those would just suit me . . ." Then he said:

"There'd even be room for the Rocket Racer . . .?"

Kim's heart leapt. It was just what she and Andy were thinking! She stared at her mother pleadingly.

"Well . . . I . . . It's very difficult. I don't want to be rushed. I was thinking more of Uncle *Ronald*. . ."

"Please . . . PLEASE – Mum . . ."

Poppy began to bristle and look all angry and flustered. "Stop trying to wheedle me round. How can I promise anything? Those garages are a complete mystery to all of us. And anyway it depends on Ronald."

Kim gave a small jump in the air, and a small half-hidden clap of her hands. She knew her mother was beginning to melt at last. And Mr Proud beamed happily because he knew it, too.

Slowly but surely the wheels were beginning to move . . .

4   A Couple of Frights

"We've got the garages!" Mr Proud's voice
boomed the news so loudly it echoed all round
Peeling Tower.

"I saw Councillor Jones about them," he said
to Kim and Andy. "Councillor Jones said he
didn't even know they were empty, and that
everybody thought everyone else was using
them."

Kim and Andy were training and training –
ready for the first Peeling Tower cycle event.
Things couldn't have been better. Mr Proud was
planning a really good circuit and the weather
forecast was good weather – for ages . . .

Every single day they timed each other to see
how long it took to race up the quiet road to The
Everything Shop and back. They used a large
pocket watch with a seconds hand you could stop
and start. Sometimes Andy went faster, and
sometimes Kim did.

Kim could hardly wait for the day when their

own real race would take place.

"There'll be a lot of competition," said Andy. "Loads of people have said they'll enter, and most of them are older than we are . . ."

"I'm glad mum knows about it all at last," said Kim as they walked away from the two garages for about the millionth time because they just couldn't believe their luck. "It seems too good to be true." Kim said. Then – as they got back on their bikes for yet another training run she said: "The very next thing I'm going to do is to cut my hair very short and shave my legs. Lots of men shave their legs. They think it makes them move quicker."

Andy slowed down in horror: "You can't do *that,*

Kim! You'll ruin everything. Your mum'll have a fit! And you haven't got big hairy legs like some of those men. It'd be different if you were in the Tour de France or something . . . And your hair's all right. Lots of people have long hair to do cycle racing. It'll make your mum even *more* against it!"

"I don't care!" Kim's voice rose dramatically: "I want my hair cut really short all over, and *you* can cut it for me." They both nearly fell off their bikes this time, as they stopped by a tree. Kim nearly fell off because she was picturing herself with hair cropped into a speeding, winning, star style. And Andy nearly fell off from the awful sudden shock of it all – because he knew what grown-ups were like when it came to hair . . .

"I can't Kim! I can't cut hair. I tried once and the scissors went all criss-cross and didn't work. I don't want to either. You're just being plain stupid." Andy's face was dark and angry.

Kim's cheeks were scarlet. So why was it stupid because she – a girl – wanted to shave her legs and get her hair cropped?

"I never am being stupid. You *like* men with short hair and you *love* that swimmer who hasn't got any hair at all . . ." her eyes flared dangerously. "If you don't cut it – I'll find someone else – and if I don't find someone else I'll do it!"

Andy looked at her, perplexed. Every so often she had ideas that caused trouble . . . and this was one of them. Just when everything was working out nicely. What a time to be awkward!

"You wouldn't catch me, shaving *my* legs," he said. "Hairs on legs are there to protect us. They carry air across the skin and they keep dust off. Hair on legs is a good idea. And you can hardly *see* them!"

"I'll think about it then," said Kim. 'I'll just rub that wintergreen stuff on them, instead . . ." Then she smiled. The outburst was over. "Perhaps you're right about legs, Andy, but I'm definitely cutting my curls off."

"Kim? What are you doing?" Her mother's voice was sharp. Almost as sharp as the scissors in Kim's bedroom.

Her thin straggling curls had vanished. Well, not quite – for they lay scattered in an untidy trail across the bedroom carpet. And now, as she stared through the small mirror above the chest of drawers, a strange urchin gaped back at her with chunky, lumpy, hacked-off hair which stuck out in short spiky tufts all over her scalp like the bristles of an old sweeping brush . . .

What on earth had she done?

The trouble was that, once she'd started, she always found a little bit she'd missed until in the end her hair was as short as a moth-eaten mat.

She felt quite alarmed now. How in heaven's name was she going to face her mum?

Supposing her mother fainted on the spot at this awful sight? If that happened she would have to give her plenty of fresh air and loosen all tight clothing . . .

"KIM! Did you *hear* me?"

In a sudden panic she tugged the pillow case from her pillow and put it on her head so that just her face and the bottom tips of her ears showed. And not a moment too soon.

The door shot open and her mother burst in: "What *are* you up to?"

Then to her relief and before her mother had time to spot scissors, or hair on the floor – the door bell rang. Saved by the bell . . .

"Ronald . . . what a nice surprise . . . you didn't go to play cricket then?"

Kim groaned: Uncle Ronald too! Both of them. She took the pillow case off and found a blue woolly cap with a bobble on it that she usually wore in the depths of winter. She put it on.

She slipped quietly towards the front door: "I'm just popping to Andy's"

"Don't be too long then dear," said her mother as she told Ronald all about the new garage for his car.

"What's that you've got on?" said Andy. "Aren't you boiled?"

"I'll show you in a minute. But it'll have to be in a secret place behind the trees. I want you to tell me what it really looks like . . ."

"You mean that woolly cap?"

"I mean my *hair* . . . I've cut it. It's hidden under this – " Slowly, behind the biggest beech tree they could find, Kim removed the blue woolly cap: "There! What do you think?"

"It's a bit – " Andy stopped. He couldn't quite find the right words.

"Go *on* then . . . The main thing is – does it look all right for cycle racing?"

"No one would see it – because of your crash hat. Yours looks a bit *spiky* . . . Could you flatten it with water?"

"Can you tell it's still *me*?" said Kim anxiously.

He nodded and smiled. "It's quite good now I'm getting used to it. You'll look really special when we have that race." Then he said: "I'm glad I'm not you though – your mum'll hit the ceiling."

Kim moaned: "That's the only trouble . . . Uncle Ronald's there, now – and I don't know whether to go back and face them *both*, or keep wearing this woolly cap and just letting mum see it gradually . . ."

"Shall I come back with you, now?" said Andy. "If I'm there it won't be as bad. They're never as bad when other people are there. My mum's just the same. It'll get it all over and done with quicker."

He began to ruffle up his own hair: "I'll just nip in and get a bit of Uncle Fred's hair cream and spike mine up to look like yours. Then your mum'll be able to shout at both of us and it won't be as bad as if you were on your own."

"You're a *real* friend, Andy," said Kim. "I don't feel half as bad, now."

A few minutes later Andy appeared with his hair looking like a spiky black scrubbing brush. Kim smiled at him gratefully. As they reached her flat she said: "Now for it . . . Count ten and wait for the explosion."

Everything was calm. Her mum and Uncle Ronald were sitting lovingly on the sofa.

Then slowly the scene in front of them began to sink in.

"What *on earth*," gasped her mum, "have you done to your hair? You both look like a couple of scarecrows pulled through a hedge backwards." She gazed at Kim in horror: "Yours looks as if it's all been cut off in *large* chunks!"

"It's a new style," said Andy bravely. "Some people dye it orange."

Kim stared down at the carpet: "It's only been *trimmed* a bit, mum."

"Nice and cool for summer, anyway," said Uncle Ronald, trying to make the best of it. "It wouldn't do if everyone looked the same. And cutting her own'll cost you a heck of a lot less in hairdressers, Poppy."

"You must never, *never* do that again," simmered Poppy angrily. "If Uncle Ronald hadn't been here – I'd . . . I'd . . ." she was beaten. Her

voice petered out to dead silence.

The battle was won! A truce was declared. Uncle Ronald offered to donate some expensive hair oil to get their hair looking good again and her mum never said another word.

"Thank goodness you were there," said Kim to Andy, later. Then she whispered mischievously: "Thank goodness I've got a cycle racing hair-cut. It feels great!"

And that night as she glanced in the mirror she said to herself: "Yes, it's still me. Still me for ever!"

Then she jumped into bed in blissful happiness and fell fast to sleep.

The next day it was all "go". Mr Proud announced that the garages were ready for use – providing everyone did their share of sweeping out, scrubbing, and moving of age-old rubbish such as ancient newspapers covered in black car oil; battered old biscuit tins with rusty nuts and bolts in, and an old pram with bits of coal at the bottom of it, plus seventeen whisky bottles (all empty).

Everyone who happened to be around joined in. And Mr Bosky who was passing by insisted that the whisky bottles were valuable antiques and that he was going to store them in the hut on his allotment.

Then he turned to Kim and Andy and said: "You'll be needing to get your bike out of the hut this morning. I didn't bring it over to Mr Proud's for you today. This'll be its last night of staying there now it's got this proper home. So maybe you could take these empty bottles with you and get your bike at the same time. Put the bottles in the hut and lock the place up again for me."

They both nodded enthusiastically. They had never ever collected the bike before. Mr Bosky always brought it in and out of the hut himself. He left it with Mr Proud almost every day. He said that some of the other allotment holders didn't like to see strange children mooching about round their vegetables, and also he wouldn't like the key to his hut to get lost. But as this was the very last time . . . it was different.

"It's almost like a sort of ceremony isn't it?" said Kim as she and Andy carried the bottles carefully in two large shopping bags, towards the broad, white, wooden farm gate where the allotments were, just behind the housing estate.

There was a big board up at the entrance. It said: "No unauthorised person may enter these allotments".

"Are we 'Unauthorised'?" asked Kim.

They both looked puzzled.

"I think we're all right," said Andy, "because Mr Bosky told us to come and he's given us the key to his hut."

Most of the allotments were very neat. They were in long strips with a path running in between

NO UNAUTHORISED
PERSON MAY
ENTER THESE
ALLOTMENTS

them, and every so often there were pipes with taps on the end where people could go for water to water plants. Some people had greenhouses on their allotments and some people had almost made their huts into little homes with curtains at the windows. Everywhere there were rows and rows of potatoes, cabbages, peas, brussel sprouts, onions, runner beans, broad beans and lettuces; and here and there a good clump of rhubarb or a row of colourful sweet-peas.

"Isn't Mr Bosky's *neat?*" said Kim admiringly, as they stared at the long strip of land in front of them filled with rows of thriving, weedless vegetables. A small cedar-wood hut stood at the far end. Carefully they trod along the side of the vegetables to the hut, still carrying the bags of empty bottles.

"I'll be glad to get rid of these," said Andy as he plonked his bag down so they could open the hut door.

"Mind where you're putting it," warned Kim. "I've already trodden on some of Mr Bosky's mint by accident and I think there's parsley right where you've put that bag. It's bright green frilly-looking stuff . . . I'm glad we've never been before or Mr Bosky wouldn't have any plants left . . ."

She began to fit the key into the door of the hut. Then she stopped: "That's funny . . . It's just not working."

"Here, let me try." Andy took the key and tried

to turn it in the lock – but it wouldn't budge. "Mr Bosky must have given us the wrong key," he said.

It suddenly began to dawn on them . . .

"I hope we're on the right allotment," said Kim slowly. "But I'm sure this is the one Mr Bosky said . . ."

"We can soon check up by looking through the hut window," said Andy. The windows were small and high up.

"If we stood on that bin thing over there with the lid on it we could soon see if the bike's there," said Kim.

The bin she'd seen was a green one. They opened the lid and peered in. There were some big, heavy stones in it. They didn't dare take them out because they knew they were the sort of thing not to be touched by strangers. But . . . my godfathers . . . the weight of that bin! Kim felt as if she would explode as she helped Andy to push, pull, drag, and heave it towards the hut so that they could climb on it to look through the hut window.

"Phew . . ." breathed Andy as they both balanced on it together.

And then it happened . . . It was as if the heavens had opened. It was like getting a slap in the back with a wet cloth. They gasped and fell from the bin lid, as a great sheet of water completely drenched them.

They picked themselves up off the ground like a pair of drowned rats. An elderly man was standing there holding a bucket. He was scowling like thunder. "You'll nae find 'owt in there – y'little villains! Be off wi'ye – 'affore a'gets hose pipe on ya!"

Without waiting a second longer they turned and ran away, yet all the time Kim was thinking about her bike. The man was so fierce he'd even frightened them away from her own prized possession. They'd have to go back without her Rocket Racer. Then – just supposing Mr Bosky had now gone out somewhere and they couldn't tell him what had happened? It might mean that they wouldn't be able to get the bike for ages. And *that* meant less practise for the race. It was crucial to have her bike in its new home in the garage as soon as possible!

Her mouth was dry with disappointment. Who would have dreamed that a simple trip to Mr Bosky's allotment could end like this?

Her thoughts were halted by a sharp cry. It was the man calling them. "Come back here – the pair o'ye. And tak' this rubbish!"

"He must mean the bottles," gasped Andy, as they turned and went back towards him.

By now the man was holding one of the whisky bottles and looking at it in surprise and when they got to him he seemed quite good-tempered.

"These are very, very old . . ." he said.

"We know," said Kim breathlessly, "Mr Bosky said they were. He says they're antiques and he wants us to put them in his hut . . . and collect our bike at the same time," she added hurriedly.

"Bosky? Mr Bosky, the insurance agent? The one who grows leeks? Him as 'as the allotment next door but one?"

They looked across and saw Mr Bosky's allotment at last. It was full of rows of leeks. It was a bit untidier than this one in places. There was a big "B" whitewashed on his small green hut and as they walked over to it they could see tyre marks on the path Mr Bosky used. They were the marks of a Rocket Racer.

Kim put the key in the hut door. It turned easily. The man who'd thrown the bucket of water over them began to shuffle about a bit. "Sorry I was a bit hasty . . ." he said, "but we gets some rum little devils round here at times."

"Surely you haven't been for a swim, as well?" said Mr Bosky when they got back to Peeling Tower and gave him back the key to his hut.

They both looked at each other. Should they tell him?

Kim spoke first. She said: "Not exactly a *swim* but we had a bit of water trouble. Thank you very, very much Mr Bosky for looking after Rocket Racer with Mr Proud. I hope all the leeks you grow will make you champion of the world." Everyone laughed.

Then Mr Bosky said: "I've got a large bottle of pop here, let's drink to the cycle champions of Peeling Tower instead."

"Everything . . . every single thing is just perfect at last," thought Kim happily as she and Andy carried her bike into the first of the newly prepared garages. It looked frail there lying against a wall on its own – next to Mr Proud's work-bench. Then Mr Proud handed her a key: "It's the key to this garage. Get your mum to put it on a special hook, and don't lose it."

Kim thanked him about twenty times!

"I doubt if Poppy will ever thank me as much as that," smiled Mr Proud ruefully. But he was pleased.

"It's been a good day – in spite of getting drenched," said Andy. "And now – all we need is to win all the races on our Day of Days."

And they both waved their arms in the air in triumph.

5 Fame and Glory

The grand cycling Junior Gala Day was nearly here. The tension was terrific. It was the talk of not only Peeling Tower, but Barnfield housing estate and all the places round it.

Every day for the past week Kim and Andy had practised their cycling early in the mornings and after school in the afternoons. Then – to Kim's dismay and misery – the worst happened . . .

"Missing?" said Mr Proud. "Your wonderful new bike that we've all nursed and nurtured and fought for. Missing? Are you quite sure?"

Kim was almost fit to cry: "It was here five minutes ago, Mr Proud. It was just outside the main doorway next to that rose bush." Her voice cracked with disappointment: ". . . Just when we'd got everything right . . ."

Mr Proud sighed and put down his green felt-tipped pen. He was making one of the posters for the Gala day. It said: "CYCLE RACING. Juniors 8 – 12 handicap".

"Maybe it's just been moved. Do you think one of the younger children went away with it? There's that one who wandered off with Kerrie Thomas's dolls' pram, and young Dale's trike."

Kim shook her head. *Crash . . .!* Her cycle stardom was at an end before it had even started – in a mere time span of five careless minutes! "It's not him, he's on holiday in Blackpool."

"You look as if you've swallowed twenty pence and found a farthing," said her mum later that day. "You and Andy have been prowling about with faces as long as lamp posts . . ."

"Rocket Racer's *gone*." Tears began to fill her

eyes. "It's vanished. It's the end of *everything*. How can I ever be a racing cyclist without a *bicycle*!" Blinded by tears she rushed to her bedroom and slammed the door in grief and frustration.

Her mum just sat there at the table and gazed at the uneaten lemon meringue pie. Then she called weakly, "Can't you do *running* instead?" And when Ronald came round she said: "She hasn't had a bite to eat and she's breaking her heart over that awful bike. I wish she'd never found it in the first place. Why can't she be a runner?" Poppy's fringe quivered above her frowning eyebrows.

Andy was as upset as Kim. He walked round and round the paths and looked carefully on every bit of a tip and under bushes and in the long grass.

Suddenly he saw Kerrie Thomas running towards him.

"Are you still looking for that bike?" she yelled. "Because there's a whopping big kid wheeling it up beyond the tower. I can't stop. I'm on an urgent message for Granny."

Andy rushed along the winding path to a short cut where the path led towards the town. And sure enough in the distance was a tall thin boy. He was bending down looking at the wheel of the bicycle he was holding.

"If he gets on it and rides I'll have lost him for ever . . ." breathed Andy. But luck was on his side. The boy never even looked up as he approached.

Puffing and panting and gasping, Andy stopped next to him. "You've taken the wrong bike. It isn't yours!"

The boy looked up at last. He was about fourteen with thick brown curly hair. "Not mine?" his face looked like thunder. "Thank you *very* much for that information. Who told you *that* load of codswallop?"

"No one told me. Rocket Racer belongs to my friend! It just went missing."

The boy grinned sarcastically: "Went missing did it? Well it just so happens, titchy, that this bike went missing from the tip by the trees ages ago, and I've only just found it again. And *where* did I find it?" He scowled angrily. "Lying there as large as life at the door of the thieves' den in Peeling Tower."

"It's not a thieves' den! That bike was dumped as scrap!"

"Oh *no* . . . No *way* . . . That bike was promised *me* by Mr Munchington. He said he'd leave it there for me to pick up. He often finds odds and ends when he travels about – so he just dumps them for me and a few mates. Stuff that other people might call rubbish . . ." The boy got a bit friendlier. "It's all casual like, with Teddy Munchington. It's take it or leave it. He never bothers after he's dumped things. It's just that he likes doing some of us kids a good turn from time to time . . ."

Andy stared silently. He didn't know what to say. It all sounded quite true. There was nothing to stop Mr Munchington leaving stuff for other people to collect. But what about *Kim's* Rocket Racer? It was a proper bike now, not just a scrappy wreck.

"So what happens now, then?" he asked slowly.

"What *happens* is, I sell it – don't I? It's too small for me, anyway I've got a lightweight racer at home."

"How much do you want for it?" Andy's heart sank.

"As much as I can get," said the boy cheerfully.

"Is fifty pounds enough?" said Andy looking down at the grass.

"FIFTY POUNDS? You're *cracked*! Where's a little kid like you going to get fifty pounds?"

Andy wished he'd never said it. He could never get fifty pounds in a month of Sundays. Something had driven him to say it – just to see what the boy would do.

The boy began to scratch his head and look restless. Then he gave the Rocket Racer a slight kick and said: "Five quid's more like it. And I'll bet you've not got more than five pence!"

Andy nodded. He felt better: "Two pence," he said.

The boy suddenly smiled good-naturedly, and taking the bike he picked it up in the air and with all his strength he hurled it into some rough grass.

It landed with a huge clanging crash as if all the spokes had been knocked flying. "Take it then! I'm fed up with it. Take it for nowt' and think yourself lucky . . ." Then turning away without another word he made for the main road and was gone for ever.

Andy couldn't believe his luck! He went to the bike and tried to lift it but the wheel was buckled again from being thrown so heavily.

"It's ours again, though . . ." he thought.

Half wheeling it, half dragging it, he struggled back to Peeling Tower. It took him *ages* and often he felt like throwing the bike back in the grass again.

Then he suddenly saw Kim. She was rushing headlong towards him – her face bright with joy: "I saw you from the window! Where . . .? How did you find it?"

After he'd told her he said: "It'll need mending all over again."

"But it's *back* . . . that's the main thing. Here, let me drag it for a bit. You have a rest."

Just as they reached the door of Peeling Tower who should be coming through but Mark Macdonald's father.

"What's up?" said Wally. "Been in a bit of trouble?" And when they explained, he said: "Worse things happen at sea. Leave it with me for a couple of days and I'll see what I can do. I'll get you a safety chain for it an' all . . ."

"All's well that ends well, then," said Mr Proud when they told him. "Now, you can both settle down and help me with these posters for the Gala."

"We found it!" called Kim when she got home again. "I'll eat *all* that lemon meringue pie, now."

"Too late my girl. Uncle Ronald's eaten it."

But Kim could tell her mum was glad things were right again.

"We're in a heat wave!" said Mr Proud on Gala Day. "The hall barometer is high and steady." His nose shone in the brilliant sunshine.

Kim, Andy, Mark and Kerrie had worked hard with the posters. There were posters about the cycle race on garden gates, in shop windows and on notice boards.

Mark's dad had persuaded his friend, champion top racer and cycle shop owner, Jack of Wheeler's Corner, to donate some prizes.

Kim's face glowed as she studied the list.

1st prize: Special Peeling Tower sweat shirt.
           Donated by Jack of Wheeler's
           Corner.
2nd prize: Bicycle Hip Flask.
           Donated by Jack of Wheeler's
           Corner.

Jack of Wheeler's Corner was really generous. The list seemed to go on for ever: racing hats, track mitts, bike re-sprays, and shopping vouchers. And then Kim saw: "Four prizes of fifty pence each for lap winners – donated by Granny Thomas of Peeling Tower. A puncture repair kit: Best youngest cyclist – donated by Mr Proud – Race organiser. And finally: One pair of white socks donated by Mr and Mrs Bosky for The Most Unfortunate Rider . . .''

"There are twenty-eight people going in for it," said Andy. "I never dreamed we'd get so many! And three more girls too, Kim. Two of them are *huge*. They look about fourteen but they're only supposed to be eleven."

She nodded quickly: "And did you see Jeff Sparkey? His legs are as long as pine poles. But perhaps it'll take them longer to pedal than with short legs like ours." Then she said: "I hope we win something for the honour of Peeling Tower. And I hope Rocket Racer doesn't fall to bits. And I hope I don't fall off!"

"It'll be stronger than ever now it's been mended again," said Andy, staring at her racing outfit. "Fancy your mum buying you that. It looks fantastic!"

"It was Uncle Roland. He said if I was racing I might as well do it in style. Yours is good, too Andy. Red, green and white make you look like a proper champion. Come on – let's go and get our bikes checked over . . . All us young ones are being given a three-minute start on the older ones."

Kim's heart thumped as she put on her crash hat – supposing she actually won one of those laps round Peeling Tower? The whole race was quite long. They all went round in a circle, four times. It was nearly five miles all together.

Suddenly she noticed everything going very quiet . . .

It seemed strange . . .

Some of the entrants were even whispering and muttering as they wheeled their bikes to the starting line. Then she saw Andy feeling his bike tyres suspiciously.

"Just checking . . ." said Andy, slowly. "There's a rumour going round there may be trouble."

"Trouble?" Kim stared at him anxiously. Why oh *why* didn't things go smoothly all the time? How could there possibly be trouble when everything had been so well organised?

"Mrs Spike . . ." muttered Andy, giving her a knowing, desperate look.

"Not *here*?"

Andy nodded. "Someone's seen her. She always tries to cause trouble. It started twenty years ago when Mr Robson the Lord Mayor ran into the back of her car. He was on his tandem with his wife."

But Mrs Spike was soon forgotten as they hurried to the starting line, and the first group of riders set off, followed a bit later by the next group.

Kim was at the front. She pushed on relentlessly, pedalling like fury up hills and round corners, along the winding hummocky track; guiding the

Rocket Racer skilfully and keeping with a bunch of four other riders.

And – wonder of wonders – towards the end of the first time round she was still at the front.

"Kim's winning the first lap!" shouted someone. But soon it began to get much harder. More and more people were catching up and overtaking her.

Then – to her astonishment she saw all the front ones slowing down. Some of them even began to *get off their bikes!* For, in front of all the racers, completely blocking the path like a great woolly blanket was a large flock of comfortable, unperturbed sheep idly wandering hither and thither and occasionally bleating.

The place was in complete chaos. And in the middle of all the chaos was Mrs Spike in an orange raincoat and green wellies (even though it was boiling hot!)

"She's let those sheep out of Lostock's field on purpose!" said someone above all the howls of disappointment.

But a few seconds later Farmer Lostock arrived with his sheep dogs Angel and Mercy – and although he seemed very slow amongst all the mix-up – a couple of whistles later the flock were in an orderly procession scuffling back to their own field.

Soon all the racers were away again. But by now Kim was a long way back and Andy was well to the front.

"I must get to the front again . . . I must . . . I *must!*" She put every drip and drop of energy she could find into harder and harder pedalling.

At last she began to gain ground. At last, with her teeth in an air-gasping, grimacing smile of agony, the sweat pouring from her forehead she began to grind creepingly to the front again in one last painful effort until she was almost level with the huge speeding bodies of gigantic Maisie Lee (who wasn't really *that* big . . .) and panther-like Becky Bell, two of the girls ahead.

But *still* the battle wasn't won.

Maisie and Becky were suffering as well and they began to speed up the pace.

"I hate cycle racing. I *hate* it! Why am I doing it?" Kim's heart was thumping. She no longer felt happy. She felt tired and miserable and exhausted as she actually *passed* Maisie and Becky and caught up with Andy – yet feeling like packing the whole thing in any minute. By now she was deaf to all the cheering people, and never even saw her mum and Uncle Roland sitting there in garden chairs licking choc-ices.

"Come on! Keep going! You're all great!" roared Mr Proud. "Only one more lap to go and not a single drop-out."

Then – on that very last lap – just as Kim was getting close to the top three riders (who were all much older and went on cycling holidays to places like Majorca) she felt her front tyre begin to go

down . . . Wobble, wobble . . . thump, thump, thump . . . thump . . . thump.

Her luck had run out.

With an almost breaking heart she wheeled her bike off the circuit lane. Her eyes felt hard and gritty and dry with bitter grief. It wasn't *fair* – after all that effort – all that trying – and all that pain – And look where it had got her. Coming in *last* with a puncture!

Slowly she walked to the finishing tape and heard people shouting and clapping as the winners rode in, in triumph.

Then she saw Andy.

"A puncture . . ." she could hardly gulp the words.

Andy hardly said anything. Then he said: "It even happens to world champions. And you won the first lap – which is more than me. I was up near the front but I came eleventh so I missed a prize." He suddenly smiled with happiness: "It was great though wasn't it?"

She sighed . . . then smiled a bit herself: "I suppose so. Better luck next time . . ."

Next time? What had she said?

"I was *nearly* thinking of packing up for ever . . ."

"But you aren't are you?" said Andy anxiously. "We can soon mend the puncture. In long races they mend them and keep on racing."

Kim shook her head and actually laughed: "I can't pack up now! Not after actually *passing*

Becky Bell and Maisie Lee!"

The wooden platform for the prize-giving was just outside Peeling Tower. Wally and Mr Proud had made it.

Mr Proud was announcing the winners.

"We'll start in reverse order," he said: "So the last prize of a pair of white socks – donated by Mr and Mrs Bosky for The Most Unfortunate Rider goes to Kim – our star junior, and star rider over all who unfortunately punctured."

She could hardly believe her ears. Mr Proud had called her the STAR RIDER! People were cheering and clapping.

"Go on then," urged Andy. "Go up and get your prize. Don't just *stand* there in a dream!" Then he said: "It's a pity I wasn't the youngest rider," as he saw Mark Macdonald going up to receive the puncture outfit. "We could have just done with it."

"We enjoyed it all very much, dear," said Kim's mum the next day. "Better than I thought. Glorious weather and as smooth as clockwork."

Kim drew a deep breath: Smooth as clockwork? Sheep all over the track? *A puncture* at the crucial winning moment: Calm . . . *Cool?* SMOOTH? But this time she didn't say anything – she just smiled.

Then she said: "When you get married to Uncle Roland, can we go the France to watch the *Tour de France?*"

And for once her mum didn't actually say no.

"We'll think about it," she said. "Yes . . . we'll certainly think about it; now you're the Cycle Star of Peeling Tower . . ." and they hugged each other.